A Story About Social Anxiety

Marjie Braun Knudsen & Jenne R. Henderson, Ph.D.

Summertime Press

Published by:
Summertime Press
Beaverton, Oregon
www.summertimepress.com

The concepts and ideas presented in this book are not intended
as a substitute for professional help. This book is a work of fiction.
All names, characters, and events portrayed in this book are the
product of the author's imagination. Any resemblance to any event
or actual persons is unintended.

ISBN: 978-0-9815759-0-2

Publisher's Cataloging-in-Publication
(Provided by Quality Books, Inc.)

Knudsen, Marjie Braun.
   BRAVE : be ready and victory's easy : a story about
   social anxiety / by Marjie Braun Knudsen & Jenne R.
   Henderson.
      p. cm.
   SUMMARY: A young boy learns to manage his fears of
   social situations and criticism. He uses the acronym
   BRAVE, which stands for "be ready and victory's easy,"
   to plan ahead for difficult situations.
   Audience: Grades 3–8.
   ISBN-13: 978-0-9815759-0-2
   ISBN-10: 0-9815759-0-0

   1. Social phobia—Juvenile fiction. [1. Social phobia
—Fiction. 2. Anxiety—Fiction. 3. Fear—Fiction.]
I. Henderson, Jenne R. II. Title. III. Title: Be ready
and victory's easy : a story about social anxiety.
IV. Title: Be ready and victory is easy.

PZ7.K783Bra 2008   [Fic]
                    QBI08-600102

| Table of Contents |

| Prologue |

My name is Danny, and I'll admit that not so long ago, I did not like school. So much could go wrong that it gave me a stomachache or a headache. I worried about messing up a project, getting called on in class, thinking kids would laugh at me or pick on me—the list went on and on and on. Then, in fifth grade, life started to change.

Chapter 1

School

"Hey, Danny!" yelled my classmate Jack one morning. He tripped into the room and his books went flying. Several kids in the class started laughing. I froze.

Jack jumped up and said, "Whoops, my bad," and bent over to pick up his books. Then he stood up too fast and hit his head on a cupboard. A few more kids saw this and cracked up. Jack just absently rubbed the back of his head and went to his desk.

Jack was the clumsiest and funniest boy in school. He was also the tallest. He said he wasn't clumsy; his arms and legs just tended to get in the way. People laughed at him, and he didn't seem to care. Anything could be a joke to Jack. He often had the whole class plus the teacher laughing.

Jack seemed to like school. Not me. School was full of unexpected disasters waiting to happen. We weren't allowed to talk to our neighbors in class, and the teacher was always telling us to listen because she'd only give the directions once. When I went down to the bathroom one time while she explained a writing assignment, I totally missed what she'd said. I wasn't about to ask anybody, so I guessed and did the project wrong.

Another day, though I worked really hard on my math worksheet, I couldn't find it. I emptied out my desk completely. It wasn't anywhere! The whole thing had to be done over. Later, I found it smashed at the bottom of my backpack, but it was too late.

Playing outside wasn't even any fun. Whenever this guy named Sam joined in a basketball game, he'd hit me. He thought he was being funny, but it hurt, and I hated playing with him. I was afraid to say anything, 'cause the other kids would think I was a wimp. The only time school was a tiny bit fun was when I got to hang out with my best friend, Tiago. But he'd been sick a lot lately, and then I was on my own.

I would do anything to get out of school. I had tried faking sick or hurt to get out of it. The time we had to do a book report, I missed a whole week. Mom didn't fall for the sick routine anymore, though. A couple days here and there really added up. Ever since she saw on my report card that I missed twenty-one days the year before, she'd been on my case. I was stuck.

Things were bad enough; then our teacher, Mrs. Baker, made school a nightmare! She told us we had to get up in front of the class and give a speech. It was to last five to seven minutes. *I must get out of this!* I thought. Then she mentioned a golden opportunity.

There was one chance to get out of giving the speech—winning the science project contest. The winners would get a really nice trophy and, the very best thing of all, they wouldn't have to give the speech! *Everyone wants to win this,* I thought. *I have to win this!*

At least I had tonight to try and come up with a plan.

Chapter 2

Bus Stop

I woke up the next day and racked my brain, trying to remember what day it was. *Ugh,* I thought, when I realized it wasn't the weekend yet. I hadn't been able to come up with a plan for winning the science contest. My stomach was already beginning to hurt.

From the noise in the kitchen, I could tell Mom was making Grandma's special biscuits, my favorites. I hoped I could eat. I jumped out of bed and threw on jeans and my lucky sweatshirt. I was already worrying about the bus. What if Tiago was sick today?

After breakfast, I decided to hit my mom up for a favor. I tried to look pitiful and pleaded, "Mom . . . please take me to school. I'll wash your car. I'll vacuum the house. I'll do anything!" Dad used to drive me every day, but he left for work too early now and couldn't.

"I'm sorry, Danny," Mom said. "You need to get used to riding the bus. I can't today anyway; I'm running late. Hurry up now. Have a good day." She pushed me out of the house and practically shut the door in my face.

It was never a good day on the bus. We're the last stop, so it was always crowded by the time I got on. The kids I knew were already sitting by someone, so I could never find a seat. When the bus driver yelled, "Sit down now!" I sat in whatever seat was closest. The person sitting there usually looked annoyed.

I approached the bus stop very carefully. If I saw Sam, I was going to wait up a bit. I don't think anyone taught him that if you can't say something nice, you shouldn't say anything at all. He always has these rotten things stored up in his mouth, just waiting for someone to hurl them at. And that someone is usually me.

Sometimes I'm lucky and Tiago beats me to the stop. I wish we could walk to the bus together, but he lives in the other direction. When Tiago is around, Sam isn't as mean.

As I approached, I didn't see Tiago, and the bus would be here any minute. Some kids were playing tag, and so was Sam. *Maybe he won't bug me,* I hoped.

My neighbor Katie ran up and tagged me.

"I'm not playing," I said.

"Oh, sorry!" She hurried off to tag someone else.

Sam noticed me and yelled, "He's too much of a wuss to play! Right, Danny?"

I stood there like a dummy, staring down at my shoes, wishing he would go away. I felt my face turn red and my heart start racing. Like magic, Tiago finally showed up.

"What are you doing, Sam?" Tiago asked as he walked over to me. "Not everyone wants to play your stupid games!"

Sam knew better than to argue with Tiago, so he went back to the game. Then the bus showed up. Tiago and I got seats across the aisle from each other.

I was glad he was here. I hadn't eaten much breakfast, and lunch would've been rough without Tiago.

| Chapter 3 |

Partners

The next day we found out who our partner would be for the science project. Mrs. Baker started listing which kids would work together: "Tiago and Ellen; Sara and Michelle . . ."

Maybe I could win the contest if I got paired with Mark! He was the smartest boy in class. *Oh, please, please, please . . .* Mrs. Baker continued, ". . . Katie and Rafiq; Jack and Danny . . ."

NO! Oh, no! Jack would just want to joke about everything and not take it seriously. I already had enough trouble. "And the last group will be Mark and Maya."

What was I going to do? Mark and Maya were the *two* smartest kids in class. Maybe one of them would get sick, and they wouldn't be able to finish in time. I'd have to come up with the best idea and get my parents to help. I thought about the speech I might have to give. *Winning this science contest is the most important thing in my life!*

" . . . so get with your partner and start planning," said Mrs. Baker.

Uh-oh. Worrying about everything in my head had distracted me. I missed what the teacher was saying again. I could imagine Mom's words: "Pay attention! You spend too much time thinking about how to get out of things."

And now, here came Jack, grinning. Okay, so maybe I'd have to do all the work, but at least Jack was kind of funny. And he was always nice to me.

"Hi, Danny. What project do you want to do?" Jack asked.

"Oh, I don't know. I think I'll look for ideas on the Internet," I answered.

"Why don't we meet at my house this afternoon and try to come up with some?"

I shifted nervously on my feet. "Uh . . . I'm not sure I can. And anyway, I don't know where you live."

"My house is easy to find. I'm down the street from the school. If you can, show up around four o'clock."

I hesitated, and then said, "Okay, maybe."

It wasn't that I didn't want to go to Jack's house. I didn't like going to *anyone's* house. What if he had a big dog? I'd seen dogs almost as tall as me. What if he had mean brothers or sisters? If he had a brother like my brother, I could be in real trouble. Parents could be really scary, too, and some houses smelled weird. What if I had to go to the bathroom but didn't know where it was and had to ask? Usually, I just held it until I got home if I was in a strange place. You never knew what to expect.

I decided I'd just go home and look up stuff on the Internet. That way, I'd get some ideas without having to go to Jack's house at all. I'd rather do it on my own anyway. Then, when we got started on the project, we could work at my house. It'd be safer that way.

| Chapter 4 |

Nick

That afternoon, I dropped my backpack by the door and headed for the kitchen. Something smelled tasty and my stomach was grumbling. "Mom, I'm home!"

I could hear her yell from her office, "I'm on the phone. I'll be there in a minute."

Yes! Chocolate chip peanut butter cookies. The super-colossal ones with the gooey center. The first bite was pure paradise.

It was also the end of my enjoyment, because I could hear someone come in the front door, and I knew it was my brother, Nick.

Nick's fourteen and thinks he's really cool. We aren't exactly buddies. He seems to be bugged if I'm even in the same room with him. When he's bored he picks on me and pulls mean pranks. Once, he took apart a bunch of Oreo cookies and put garlic powder in them. He knows I love Oreos. When I went to eat some, I started gagging and threw up. He got in big trouble. That whole night I couldn't get the garlic taste out of my mouth. It was totally gross.

As soon as he walked in the room he started in on me. "Hey spaz, don't eat all the cookies."

"Don't call me spaz. And I can eat all the cookies I want."

"My friends are coming over, so don't be a pest and try to hang around us. If you do, I'll throw all your little *Game Boy* stuff in the trash."

I was getting mad. "You can't throw away my games. I'll tell Mom! You'll have to pay for them!"

Mom walked into the kitchen. "Okay, that's enough. You two need to stop this fighting."

"He said he was going to throw all my *Game Boy* stuff in the trash."

"He's so annoying, Mom. He always hangs around when my friends are over." Nick grabbed two cookies.

"He called me spaz!" I added, just to make sure he got into trouble.

"Nick, I've talked to you about name calling. It has to stop. Dad and I will be talking to you about this tonight."

Nick gave me the evil eye as he left the room, while Mom went over to the fridge. I stuck my tongue out at him.

Good. I had Mom to myself now.

She walked over to the table to pour me some milk. "You know, Danny, you don't have to respond to Nick when he picks on you. You can choose to ignore him."

"But he makes me so mad, I can't help it."

"Do you know why Nick calls you names?"

"Yeah, he's the meanest brother ever."

"Well, I think he wants to make you mad on purpose so you'll lose your cool. It makes him feel good and powerful when he can make you yell. I bet if you don't react the way he wants, he'll stop."

I thought that was dumb. There was no way Nick would stop picking on me, especially if I didn't do anything about it. Mom could see that I wasn't convinced.

She added another strategy. "Try this. Whenever Nick starts to bother you, I want you to answer him with one of two words. Either say, 'So' or 'Whatever.'"

"How will that help?"

"Well, it doesn't give him anything to argue back against. It takes two to fight, you know. If you refuse, it's over. There's no way one person can fight unless the other person joins in. Give it a try. Remember: 'So' or 'Whatever.' Okay?"

"Okay." It couldn't be worse than what I was doing now.

| Chapter 5 |

Help

"So, how did school go today?" Mom asked. "Awful. We have to give a speech, and the only way to get out of it is to win this science project contest. I got paired up with this guy named Jack. You have to help me, or Dad does. This is really important."

Mom shook her head. "You have to do the project yourself, Danny. But I'll be happy to help with ideas."

"No, you don't understand. Jack's nice, but everything is funny to him. I don't think he takes anything seriously. We'll never win by ourselves. Mark and Maya are teamed up together, and Mark always wins everything. This is life or death, Mom! You have to do it!"

"I said I'd help with ideas, but you still have to do the work yourself." Obviously, Mom didn't understand the seriousness of the situation.

"Aw, Mom. What am I going to do? Jack wants me over at his house at four o'clock to come up with ideas for our project, but I don't want to go. He won't be much help anyway."

"Well, I think you should go. You never know. He might be a harder worker than you think."

"Yeah, right!" I complained. "I don't want to go to his house. I've never been there before. I don't even know where he lives."

Unfortunately, Mom is always quick with a solution. "The directory is right here. Let's see . . . here it is. It's right over by school. I'll finish up my work and run you over."

Sometimes Mom just didn't get it! There was no way I could give that speech. And she knew I didn't like going to other kids' houses.

She made me go. I figured if I didn't like it over there, I'd say I had a headache and come home. When we pulled up to the front of his house, I was surprised. It looked really big from the front and had these cool-looking pillars. There were two little trees by the door, trimmed to look like perfect spirals. I rang the doorbell and was relieved that Jack answered the door.

"Hey, Danny!" he said as he led me in. "Welcome to the pit."

| Chapter 6 |

Jack's House

"Hey, Jack. I can't stay long, but maybe we can come up with a few ideas." I was already plotting my excuse to leave in my head.

"Fine by me. Let's go into the family room and work in there."

I followed him downstairs. There was a huge couch on one wall that looked comfy enough to take a nap in. I could hear loud snoring from the other room. It sounded frightening, and I worried about who it was.

Then I saw the TV. Wow! It was twice as big as ours at home. *Spongebob* was on, and it was my favorite episode—the one where Spongebob is the leader of the band and Squidward is the conductor. Jack must have liked it too. He said we could work in there and watch TV. He was lucky; I never got to work in front of the TV.

I asked him if his parents were home. He said they were out of town a lot, but his grandpa was always there. He was in the other room taking a nap.

So it was his grandpa in there snoring! Maybe we could get this finished up, and I could get home before his grandpa woke up. I didn't know about his grandpa, but mine was pretty grumpy around kids.

I was surprised that Jack had so many good ideas. My favorite was his plan to use little sticks to show how bridges work and which ones were strongest. The idea I had of seeing which bag of popcorn pops the most kernels didn't sound very interesting, although Jack thought it would be fun and we could eat all the popcorn.

We could hear someone moving around in the other room, and the door opened.

"Hey, Gramps, you're up," Jack said.

"Hi there, kiddo. Who's your buddy?" Jack's grandpa was a big, hairy man. He was taller than anyone I'd ever seen. He would have been very scary if he didn't have such a big smile. I liked him immediately.

"This is my science partner, Danny. We're going to win the school trophy and get out of a speech for having the best science project."

His grandpa's smile got a little bigger. "Well, isn't that swell. Those are some high stakes. You're sure welcome to use anything out in my woodshop."

Remembering my manners, I said, "Thanks, that will help. There's no way I'm going to give that speech. We've got to win."

"Why don't you want to give a speech, Danny?" Jack's grandpa asked.

He seemed nice enough, so I figured I could tell him. "Well, I hate going up in front of the class. The speech is supposed to be really long, and I don't even know what to talk about. I know I'd look stupid."

"Some things are not as bad as you think, Danny. Jack needs to tell you all about BRAVE," he said. Then he headed into the kitchen.

I asked Jack what his grandpa had meant. He explained that the letters in BRAVE stood for the first letters in the saying, Be ready and victory's easy.

"B.R.A.V.E. That's how you remember it. My gramps reminds me of it every time I do anything. It doesn't matter what it is—basketball, baseball, tests, reports, and even chores. Gramps always says, 'BRAVE applies to everything in life, Jack. If you can remember that, you'll do fine.'"

Pretty soon, I heard the sound of popcorn popping. It smelled like the buttery kind that Mom gets, the movie-theater flavor. I hoped Gramps was making it for us, because it smelled tasty.

Chapter 7

Brave

Gramps walked back into the room with a bowl of popcorn and three mugs of hot apple cider. Apple cider wasn't my favorite, but there was no way I'd say anything. I'd just met Jack's grandpa, and I didn't want to make waves by asking for something else.

Jack was saying, "Gramps and I spend a lot of time together."

"We have a lot of fun, don't we, kiddo?"

"Yep, we have a lot of fun."

After we were settled in with our snack, his grandpa started telling me about BRAVE.

"'Be ready and victory's easy.' I'll tell ya, Danny, when Jack was younger, there were plenty of times being ready brought victory. Right, Jack? Like when he first started playing soccer. The other kids teased him because he didn't understand how to maneuver the ball. Jack really wanted to play, but he worried about the other kids laughing at him. So that's when I knew it was time to tell him about BRAVE."

Jack? Worried? "What happened?"

"Tell him, Gramps," Jack said.

"The University of Portland is right here in town, you know, and their team had won the national championship in soccer. We went over to watch them practice, to see how the really great players go about it. Then we started doing soccer drills every afternoon. Once Jack got the basic skills of the game down, he was ready for soccer camp."

"That was a tough two weeks!" Jack reminisced.

"That's right," his grandpa said. "But after all that work, you were ready to play on a team, weren't you? That's all it took. A little prep work, and victory was sure easier for Jack, Danny. He ended up being one of the best players on the team, and they almost went undefeated. So, you see? Be ready and victory's easy!"

"Like I said," Jack added, "it works on everything."

His grandpa nodded. "I've seen it help Jack with school assignments and tests. Heck, his parents even use it too! When they go on a trip, they make sure they're prepared, so the trip goes smoothly. Jack's mom grew up knowing that if you can be ready, then victory's easy."

Wow, this brave stuff did sound like a good idea; but I didn't know if it'd work for me. If Jack was good at being prepared, though, we might stand a chance of winning the science contest. Maybe working with Jack wouldn't be so bad after all.

| Chapter 8 |

Practicing

When Mom picked me up, Nick was in the car too.

"Get in back and be quiet," Nick said. "I like this song."

I almost fell for it again, but Mom's voice popped into my head. I decided to try the two words she told me to use.

"Whatever."

When the song was over, Nick looked back at me and said, "Did you actually do any work over at that kid's house? I'll bet you goofed off the whole time."

"So."

"You know you won't win any science contest."

"So."

"Is that all you can say? 'So'?"

"Whatever." I turned away from him and stared out the window. I could see the corners of Mom's mouth turned up in the side-view mirror. I felt a little surge of power just then.

That night I kept thinking about Jack and Gramps. How come Jack was so happy all the time? He told me that his parents traveled for weeks at a time. He mostly only had his grandpa, although he did seem like a really nice guy. That thing Gramps said about being brave was kind of neat. I sat down at my desk to do my homework. I wrote out the reminder and put it on my bulletin board:

Be
Ready
And
Victory's
Easy

I had a spelling test the following morning, and I was getting a stomachache already. Feeling sick before every test stinks. I usually breeze through my spelling words the night before, but then I always get some wrong. My eyes wandered to the word BRAVE. Maybe if I spent a little more time practicing my spelling words, I'd be more prepared for the test. If being ready brought Jack victory, I figured I could give it a try.

This time, to be prepared, I made five copies of my word list. I taped them up above my desk, near my bed, on my door, in the bathroom, and by the refrigerator. For the rest of the day, every time I went past them, I shut my eyes and practiced spelling them. By the time I went to bed, I felt good.

The spelling test might go okay.

| Chapter 9 |

Pancakes

Mom only had to wake me up twice the next morning. I quickly got dressed and went downstairs. Something was wrong. I wasn't dreading school as much as usual.

"Hey, Mom, can I have pancakes this morning?" I asked.

"Sure." She walked over to get them out of the freezer. "I saw your words taped up here. I'm happy to see you spending some extra time on your spelling."

"Well, it's kind of Jack's grandpa's idea. I met him yesterday. He has this really cool saying. It goes, Be ready and victory's easy. The letters spell out the word "brave," so it's easy to remember. I was thinking of it when I was doing my homework."

"Jack's grandpa sounds like a very smart man."

"He's nice. He knows all about building things. And it's like he's having fun when he's helping us."

"Sounds like you're off to a good start." She pulled the pancakes out of the microwave. "Oh, I almost forgot. I wanted to let you know that Uncle Hal and Aunt Betty are coming for dinner in a couple days."

"Aw, Mom, not them. They're so old. What if they ask me a bunch of questions?"

"You'll be fine. If you want, we can practice on some questions they might ask, and you can have your answers all ready."

"Well, what do you think they might ask me?"

"They'll probably ask you about school, hobbies, or what you do for fun. So, start thinking of some answers to those things and I think you'll be covered."

I knew this would not be good. I had enough to think about with the science project, the bus stop problems, and whether or not Tiago would be at school. Now this too.

The phone rang, and Mom ran into the office to answer it.

Then Nick stumbled into the room. His hair was all messed up as if he'd just rolled out of bed. He didn't look awake yet, and Nick is twice as mean when he's tired. Great.

I didn't have to wait long.

"Loser," he said. "What are you looking at?"

I shrugged my shoulders. I did not want to get in a fight with him this morning.

He tried again. "Why aren't you saying anything, stupid? Man, what a pig. Look at all the syrup you used. Don't you know it's pure sugar? It'll rot your brain and your teeth."

"I don't care. I love pancakes dripping with syrup and tons of butter."

"Go ahead then, rot away, dork."

"Whatever."

Luckily, my breakfast was finished and my backpack was ready to go. I'd had enough of grumpy old Nick, but it wasn't as bad as usual. I was getting the hang of the "so" and "whatever" answers.

There was no more putting it off. The dreaded bus stop was waiting for me.

Chapter 10

Keep Away

There were some kids at the bus stop already, but I didn't see Sam. Maybe he was out sick. I sat on the curb and watched some kids play kick the can.

It looked like fun. I wanted to play, but I figured I'd better wait until Tiago got there.

Someone walked up behind me. Then I heard that horrible voice.

"Hey, are you frozen or what? You never play any games," Sam said.

Shoot! Where is Tiago? I glanced over my shoulder. "So," I said.

Then Sam grabbed my backpack. "Nice backpack."

I jumped up. "Stop it, Sam!"

He sneered. "Hey, Todd! Catch!" He launched my backpack.

Todd was in sixth grade and a lot taller than me, but I tried to get my backpack from him anyway. I'd get close, only to have him yank it away at the last second. Sam and Todd kept running away from me, throwing my backpack back and forth like a football.

The other kids quit playing their game and stood around watching. I could feel myself getting nervous, and I wanted to cry. *Everyone's going to think I'm such a loser!* There seemed to be no good way out of this.

Then I remembered Mom saying that Nick liked it when I lost my cool. So I decided to sit on the curb and do nothing.

Pretty soon, Sam and Todd realized I had given up. I guess it wasn't fun for them when I stopped chasing them around, so they threw my backpack on the curb and walked away, laughing. *Hey! It worked!* I thought. I wished everyone hadn't been watching, though. It made me feel stupid and like a baby.

The bus finally arrived and people ran off to get their backpacks. It was about time!

As soon as I walked into school, there was Mark talking about how great his science project was going to be. He said he was making a perfect working replica of the water cycle. He didn't *think* he was going to win, he *knew* it. Today he was even wearing a tie. What loser would dare to wear a tie to school? I heard some kids saying that they wouldn't have a chance to win.

Then I came up with a great idea. I had twenty-two dollars left of my birthday money. Maybe if I gave it to Mark, he would promise to lose the science contest. But I'd never have the guts to go and ask him. *Maybe I can get Jack to do it,* I thought. *He's not afraid of any thing.* He might even add some money of his own, so Mark would agree. Yes! It could actually work! I would ask him right away.

| Chapter 11 |

Nervous

Our math class was getting started by working on problems up on the board. The teacher was calling on one kid in each table group to go to the front of the class. I started getting nervous and a little sweaty. Whenever I had to get up in front of the class, everyone stared at me, just waiting for me to make a mistake. So I usually did. Then they probably thought I was a dummy.

Uh-oh. Our group was next, I noticed. My heart started beating faster and made me kind of dizzy. *I hate this!* I thought, looking down at my desk and slumping in my chair. *Maybe she won't call on me.*

The teacher looked over to our group, searching out her next victim. She paused, and then said, "Jack. Could you come show us the next problem?"

What a relief! My whole body felt better as my heart slowed down and the dizziness went away. I wasn't sure if I did the problem right anyway. This was why

I could *not* give the speech. I got freaked out about going in front of the class for a stupid math problem. Imagine what would happen with a whole speech! I had to win that science contest.

As Jack walked to the front of the room, Sam pushed a book out from under his desk, and Jack tripped on it. He fell on Mark's perfectly arranged desk and knocked everything over. The kids all started laughing, except for Mark. He looked mad! The teacher looked annoyed. Jack apologized and quickly helped Mark put everything back. While I would've been mortified at the laughter and angry at Sam, Jack stood up, took a bow, and proceeded to the front of the classroom.

After math we had some free time. I told Jack that it was Sam who made him trip. He didn't care. He said, "Oh, well, it was kind of fun messing up Mark's perfect desk."

"Hey, Jack, speaking of Mark, I have a great plan to beat him in the science contest."

"Sounds good. What's the plan?"

I used my most persuasive voice. "Listen. I have twenty-two dollars left from my birthday, and if you can kick in some money too, we can give him all our money if he agrees to lose. You know, he probably has plenty of trophies already. And if *you* ask him to do it, I bet he'll agree. What do you think?"

When Jack started chuckling, I knew he wasn't taking this seriously. "First of all, I want to win the science contest fair and square. Second, I only have five bucks, and I'm not giving it to Mark. And last, I think Mark is still mad at me for messing up his desk. I doubt if he would agree to it, anyway."

Well, that stunk, but I could see he was right. Now how were we going to win the science contest?

I didn't have long to think about it because the bell rang and forced me to deal with the next problem: lunch.

Chapter 12

Lunch

As I approached the cafeteria, I formed a strategy for lunch without Tiago. I'd sit at a table with only a few kids, far away from Sam. That way I wouldn't have to talk much, and Sam wouldn't be close enough to bug me. The problem was, I didn't see Sam anywhere, so I sat with some kids from my class that I knew Sam didn't hang around with.

When Tiago was here, lunch was fun. Tiago knew tons of interesting facts. He once told me that the largest living thing on the face of the Earth was right here in Oregon—a mushroom growing underground. It was three and a half miles across, and bigger than a thousand football fields. Tiago said they tested it, and it was all the same mushroom. He knew a lot because he read tons of books. It was boring without him here.

Great, here came Sam. *I'll just pretend that my food is real interesting and that I don't see him,* I thought.

"Well, if it isn't Mr. Wimpy. You gonna come out and play basketball today? Oh, wait a minute, you can't do anything without Tiago. Isn't that right?"

I tried hard to use my I-don't-care voice: "Whatever." Then I started eating, hoping he would go away.

I heard someone yell, "Sam, over here!" from across the room, and he left.

Rafiq from my class turned to face me. "He's very rude."

"I know. He's always being mean to me," I said.

"You want to hang out after lunch? We could get our own basketball game going."

"Uh . . . I don't know."

I wasn't sure what to do. Tiago wasn't here and I didn't have anyone to play with. I was planning on sitting on the steps, pretending I had a stomachache so I wouldn't have to do anything. I'd never played with Rafiq before. He was nice, but I didn't know about his friends. I decided to take the risk, since Tiago wasn't here and sitting on the steps didn't sound very fun.

After we finished eating, we all went outside. Rafiq and his friends were talking about some new computer game that I'd never heard of. I stood there and listened. One of his friends started talking about a new, rare Pokemon card he got. My collection was pretty big, but I didn't know the guy and wasn't sure I should say anything. Then he started talking about a card that he wanted, but couldn't find.

"Hey, I have that one," I blurted out before I could stop myself.

"Really? You want to make a trade?" he asked.

"Sure." I was glad to help someone out and, who knew, maybe make a new friend too. Plus, I didn't play with Pokemon cards that much anymore.

Sam walked by and heard us talking. "You babies still play Pokemon cards?" He smirked.

"So," I said.

"What a bunch of losers."

He continued on by to one of the basketball hoops. At least this time, he was making fun of others, too, and not only me. We decided to get our own basketball game going.

Playing basketball with Rafiq and his friends was fun. I missed some shots and even bounced the ball off my foot once, but nobody laughed or made fun of me. Rafiq was really cool, and his friends were nice.

| Chapter 13 |

Being Sick

After lunch, Mrs. Baker told us we were going to take some special tests for the state. They would be in reading and math. There were a lot of rules, like no looking at your neighbor's computer. And you only had a certain amount of time to finish the test, so you had to stop exactly when she said to stop. She said that these tests were important and we should do our best work.

I wasn't too happy about the state tests, and my stomach started to hurt. *Why do we need to take them anyway? They'll probably take a long time and be hard. What if I don't do good enough? I've never taken a test on a computer before. What if I mess up or make a mistake?* I didn't think I could go back and change my answer or fix it.

I hadn't been sick for a while, so maybe I could be sick on the test day.

Right before the bell rang, we got our spelling tests back. I got one hundred percent! I could *not* believe it! *Wait'll I show Mom and Dad!* I thought.

The next day, Tiago was back at school. He came home with me afterward. I was telling him that I couldn't do the state testing, so I was planning to be sick the next day. I wasn't sure how to pull it off, since I'd already tried all the usual ways to dodge school.

Tiago had a few suggestions. "You could say you have a bad stomachache and feel like you're gonna puke."

I shook my head no. "I've used the stomachache excuse too many times. It won't work anymore. I can't say my throat hurts either, because my Mom will get out the flashlight and check."

"How about if you try breathing only through your mouth, so it sounds like you have a cold? Can you do a fake cough? Go ahead, let me hear one."

I tried fake-coughing, but Tiago didn't look too impressed with my performance. I knew this wouldn't work. "It's got to be something good. I've been out sick too much this year." I was getting worried.

Tiago thought for a minute. "Okay. You're gonna need more than one symptom. Say your head hurts bad and feels like it's about to explode. But first, do a bunch of sit-ups really fast to get yourself all sweaty. Rub the bottoms of your eyes a lot so they get a little red. Then put on a jacket before you go downstairs. Tell your mom you feel really cold. Also, you should act like you can't eat any breakfast, and it would be good if you laid your head on the table."

"That's great! I haven't done all that before!"

"Hey, you might want to stock up on some snacks for your room so you don't starve. You have to keep up the no eating, or your mom might bring you in late."

"Good point. How come you know so much about faking sick?" I asked.

"I learned from the master, my older brother Juan. I save it up for when I really need a day off. If you try it too much, it doesn't work."

That was what I liked about Tiago. He didn't ask why I didn't want to take the test, or anything else. He always came through for the important stuff.

| Chapter 14 |

Bridges

It was just like Jack's grandpa said: be ready and victory's easy. The plan worked.

Staying home from school was great! I felt pretty laid-back in my cozy bed all day. My *Gameboy* was nearby, and plenty of snacks were hidden in my desk. When Mom came to check on me, I either pretended I was sleeping or squinted my eyes like my head hurt.

I knew I couldn't pull it off another day, so I didn't try. But the next day in school, my teacher said I'd have to make up the test. I couldn't believe it! After all that planning and work. Some things, it seemed, were impossible to get out of.

After school, Jack and I met at his house to work on our project. We worked in his grandpa's wood-shop. He said we could use any of his stuff. There were all kinds of tools and a million little pieces of wood. Everything was kind of dusty. Jack said that

Gramps had arthritis and couldn't use his hands for much anymore. He used to spend a lot of time in his woodshop. When Jack was little, they would spend hours building things. Gramps used to get excited over every project. Jack said he really missed that.

After several attempts at different kinds of bridges, we were getting frustrated. Everything we made broke, or wouldn't go together the way we had it planned. I was starting to panic about not ever getting it right.

"Hold on a minute," Jack said. "I'll see if Gramps will help."

Jack came back a few minutes later with some snacks and his grandpa. He didn't seem worried at all. He was eating some chips and laughing at something his grandpa said.

"Hey, Danny, have some chips. Gramps is going to tell us what we're doing wrong."

Gramps looked over our first attempts at bridge building. He said, "Well, you have the right idea. You just need to make a few structural changes."

We worked with Jack's grandpa for two hours straight. Once he explained the right way to go about it, everything seemed easier. Gramps was the nicest old guy I'd ever met. He never got mad when we did something wrong. He was always smiling and seemed like he was having fun, and it rubbed off on everyone else.

Chapter 15

Dinner

I was dreading going home, since that night my aunt and uncle were coming for dinner. Maybe I would get lucky and they wouldn't show up.

Later on at home, the doorbell rang, and I cringed. Mom and Dad made me go to answer the door.

When they came in, my Aunt Betty said the usual, "Ooh, you're getting so big!" while pulling me into a bear hug. My face was smashed into her scratchy sweater, and she squeezed me so hard, I thought I'd crack a rib.

I finally got away, only to have Uncle Hal come over and slap me on the back too hard and say, "Good man! I hope you're taking care of your mother."

After a while, we sat down to eat. Soon my uncle looked over my way. I knew what was coming—the interrogation. At least Mom had helped me get ready for the questions.

"What are you studying in school now, boy?" Uncle Hal asked.

Why does he call me "boy" anyway? He knows my name. I tried to concentrate on giving him an answer. "I'm in fifth grade now. We have all the usual subjects: math, language arts, science, and stuff."

"Well, do you know what you want to do when you grow up?"

"Uh . . . I don't know."

"Do you play any kind of sports? Football? Baseball?"

"No, I'm not really into sports. I like computer games."

My uncle looked over at my parents. He gave them a look of pity at the son that they were stuck with. Then he moved on to Nick.

"So, Nick, I hear you're quite the football player."

Nick gets interested when someone talks football. "Yeah. I'm starting quarterback on junior varsity."

"You guys winning any?"

"You bet. We're six and 0 this year, and heading into the quarter-finals."

The focus stayed on Nick for a while. Uncle Hal seemed to be only interested in sports. That was fine by me. One good thing about Nick was that he sure could talk.

Things were going okay until Mom decided to pull me back into the conversation. "Danny, tell Uncle Hal and Aunt Betty about your science project."

Of course, they both fixed their eyes on me. Great. Exactly what I didn't want to happen. What was Mom trying to do to me anyway?

I decided to get it over with. "It's no big deal. My partner and I are building wooden bridges to show which design is the strongest." I went on to explain how we first started out and some of the things that we'd learned along the way. "We're hoping to win the contest."

"Well, that sounds like quite a feat, Danny. Good luck to you."

I couldn't believe it. Uncle Hal actually seemed impressed. It wasn't so bad talking about something when I knew what I was talking about.

I survived dinner, even though Aunt Betty kept burping throughout the meal, and I was sitting right across from her. After a while, Uncle Hal let one rip, and the whole room started to reek. My uncle left to use the restroom, and my aunt said sorry for his "breaking wind" (that's what she called it). I thought it was more like "blasting wind."

When they finally left, I was extremely relieved, although it wasn't as bad as I thought it would be. It helped to be ready ahead of time.

That night when I sat down at my desk to finish my homework, I looked at the note on my bulletin board. BRAVE. Be Ready And Victory's Easy. I got all my spelling words right. Being ready did help me. Jack's grandpa knew what he was talking about. I wished he was my grandpa.

I couldn't wait to go over tomorrow to work on our project. While I was thinking about being prepared, I made sure my finished homework ended up in my folder and not smashed at the bottom of my backpack.

| Chapter 16 |

Sam

The next day, the bus arrived at school a little early. The bell rang to line up to go into class. Sam was behind me and kept pushing me. I told him to stop. Then he kept poking me. My face felt hot, and I started to tense up. I turned around again and said, "Stop!" a little louder. Those words Mom told me weren't going to work this time, not when he was pushing and poking at me. It made me so mad that I had to just stand there and take it. I wished I were big like Tiago, or clever like Jack.

Finally, Mrs. Baker showed up, and we went inside. Jack sat next to me, and we had ten minutes of free time before math.

"Hey, Jack. I want to ask you something. Sam is such a pest. Does he bug you all the time too?"

Jack said, "Yeah, I guess he used to. But I told him to stop, over and over. And I started ignoring him. I guess he got bored and stopped. He's always bugging *you* now, Danny. Tell him to stop, get away from him, and then try to ignore him. If that doesn't work, then tell the teacher. It's not worth all the hassle. Remember what my gramps says about being BRAVE. Be ready and victory's easy. Be prepared for him to be a pest and have your plan worked out. That way it will be easy to get him off your back. Victory!"

Jack kept on. "Hey, Gramps had so much fun helping us last night. I haven't seen him this excited in a long time. We have to work hard. I want to win this contest for my gramps."

"Sounds great to me! I'll be over this afternoon."

Chapter 17

To Go Or Not To Go

When I got home that day, I started working on my homework right away. I only had math to finish, and it was super easy. When I finished, I headed into Mom's office.

"Hey, Mom, can I get a ride over to Jack's house when you're done?"

"Sure, I'll be done in about a half hour," she said. "Hey, Danny, I got a call today from Rafiq's mom. She wanted to invite you to go to the corn maze with them on Saturday. What do you think?"

"Uh . . . I don't know. Rafiq is cool and all, but I've never met his family or anything."

"But you've been asking to go to a corn maze. This is a good opportunity, and Rafiq has been nice to you. It might be fun."

"I wanted to go with you and Dad. I've never been to a corn maze. I heard you can get lost and wander around for hours."

"Danny, sometimes it takes you a while to get used to something new. I have an idea. Why not try to learn more about new things, so you can get comfortable with them sooner? It's like Jack's grandpa says, 'Be ready and victory's easy.' To be ready, let's get some information."

"About the corn maze?" I asked.

"Yes. We'll look on the Internet. We can get all the details, and then you'll know what to expect. Let's see . . . it says here that the farm is in North Plains. Look at this, there's a picture of the maze. It's designed like the shape of Oregon. There's seven acres of corn. And paths that have five miles of curves, turns, loops, and dead ends."

"Five miles! That will take forever."

Mom continued her sales pitch. "It says here that to make it through the maze, kids need to find numbered signs and answer a question correctly to learn the next direction to go in."

"We'll never get out if we need to know facts and stuff," I worried aloud.

"The questions are all based on the capitals of the states. You studied them in school. That should be easy for you and Rafiq. Besides, his parents will be there too."

"Yeah, maybe." I was considering going.

"What's the worst that can happen?" Mom asked.

"I'm afraid I'll get separated from Rafiq and get lost. What if I can't find my way out?"

"Well, you tell me. What would you do if you couldn't find your way out?"

I thought about it a minute. "I don't know. I guess I would follow another group, or ask for help."

"That's a great idea. See, you do know what to do. They don't tell you this, but you can cut through the corn stalks until you reach an opening. Or start yelling until someone comes for you."

"I'm not gonna yell. That would be stupid. I didn't know you could cut through, though. I guess it might be okay."

I reluctantly agreed to go.

Chapter 18

Gym Class

Every night that week we worked at Jack's house with his grandpa. Designing bridges is a tricky task. We learned about load, width, and height of span when thinking about a bridge. You have to make sure the bridge can support itself and the mass it will be supporting. Jack's grandpa explained a lot of stuff to us, but we did all the work ourselves. It was like having our own private science coach. Our project was turning out amazing.

Later in the week, we had a blast in gym class. Learning how to juggle balls, rings, and pins wasn't as hard as I thought. I mastered the balls and was getting the hang of juggling rings when Sam came up to me with a stupid grin on his face. His hair was sticking out all over. I wondered if he ever combed it. I decided to try Jack's strategy, which I had planned out in my head.

Before he could start in on me, I calmly and firmly said, "Sam, get away. If you're going to bug me, get away." Then I took my juggling rings and walked away.

Sam followed me to the other side of the gym. I finally told the gym teacher he was bothering me. The teacher made him stay on the other side of the gym with another group of kids.

Toward the end of the school day, Mrs. Baker went over the requirements for the speech. She explained that we would eventually have to pass state benchmarks in speaking, so it was important we learn how they were scored. We would be given numbered scores based on Ideas and Content, Organization and Delivery. She emphasized the need to speak loud and clear, and to make eye contact during the speech. Gosh, I really had to get out of this! I had to win the science contest!

There was the bell. Yea, it was Friday.

Chapter 19

The Corn Maze

Mom let me take her cell phone to the corn maze on Saturday, but made me promise to keep it zipped in my coat pocket and not take it out unless I needed to. I liked knowing it was there, just in case.

Rafiq and I ran into some kids from our school at the corn maze. They asked if we wanted to race and see who could make it through first. We quickly agreed, knowing that we had all the capitals of the states memorized for the questions.

The other kids yelled "go" and took off running. We ran after them, but they were already out of sight. The questions were easy for us, so we kept working our way through the maze. It had been raining off and on for a few days, and all the paths were a slippery mush of hay and mud. A few girls followed us, since we knew the answers to the questions. Every time we got an answer right, they cheered. It was kind of fun having them on our side.

We were slipping and sliding through the maze as fast as we could. As I was going around a corner, I slipped and fell into a huge mud puddle. I was dying of embarrassment and didn't want to look up. Soon, everyone would be laughing at me.

Rafiq caught up to me and offered his hand to help me up. The girls were yelling for us to get going. I realized that the girls didn't think anything about me covered in mud; they just wanted to finish the race. So, I got up and kept going. We got to a question that stumped us.

"I can't remember the capital of Iowa," said Rafiq.

I scratched my head. "Shoot, I don't have a clue."

"My grandma's from Iowa," said one of the girls. "It's Des Moines."

We took off running again. After a lot of winding and twisting turns, and a few more questions, we finally found the exit. Everyone was excited. We didn't see the other kids anywhere, so we must have beaten them. The girls said, "Thanks!" and ran off. Rafiq helped me find the bathroom, so I could wash some of the mud off my arms.

Rafiq's parents bought some corn and apples, but they didn't go through the corn maze. They wanted to go on the hayride, though, before we went home. I'd never been on a hayride. It looked like you could fall off the wagon. I wasn't sure I wanted to go.

"Uh . . . I don't know," I said.

The guy who worked there noticed my hesitation. "What are you worried about, son?"

"What if I fall off?" I blurted out. I couldn't believe I said that to a stranger.

He said that wouldn't happen because they go so slow.

It was a bumpy ride. We went by a bunch of cows and boy did it stink! There must have been a thousand pumpkins in one field, with a few of the biggest pumpkins I'd ever seen. The road was two wheel ruts in the ground, and we kept getting stuck in the mud, but I had fun.

When we got home, I told Mom all about it. She said that maybe our whole family could go next time. Nick would for sure think the hayride was cool. I realized that I was glad I went, even though I ended up with mud everywhere, even in my underwear. I was glad Mom helped me learn about it ahead of time, so I could feel okay about going.

Chapter 20

Being Ready

It was Sunday again, the worst day of the week. I was feeling pretty good, though, since the corn maze went so great. I decided to look over my reading for tomorrow. The teacher might call on me, and I wanted to be ready.

In class the next day, the teacher said that we were going to continue reading aloud in our books. We were reading the novel *Dear Mr. Henshaw,* by Beverly Cleary. Reading aloud was bad enough, but it was worse if you stumbled on the words. Then everyone probably thought you were dumb. My turn was next, although I didn't feel as bad as usual. I rubbed my sweaty palms on my jeans and started reading.

When I was done reading, I realized that it went okay. I didn't stumble on any words. Reading ahead made me more prepared, so I didn't worry so much and get too nervous.

Katie was reading next. This part of the story had a few hard words. I hoped she'd do okay.

She read, "Mr. Fridley fastened the U.S. flag on the"—she hesitated—"hal-ee-ard? Hal-iard? Halyard. . . ."

She got tripped up, but she figured it out. No one said anything or laughed. It looked like the other kids didn't care. I thought about it. When I heard someone stumble on a word, I didn't think anything bad about them. Maybe it's okay to mess up sometimes and people won't think you're dumb.

If I ended up having to give the speech, maybe people wouldn't be paying attention. They'd probably be worried about their own speech. Okay, so if Jack and I lost, maybe it wouldn't be the worst day of my life. I still didn't want to give the speech though. We deserved to win the science contest anyway because we worked so hard.

The rest of the week went by quickly. Just about everything was set for the science project. Jack's grandpa was excited. He had promised to come to the science contest, and Jack said he never went anywhere. Jack wanted to win this so bad for Gramps, and I guess I did too. We decided that if we won, the trophy would go right on the shelf by his favorite chair.

On the way to school that evening in the car, I kept thinking about our chances of winning. "Do you think the paper I wrote is good enough? Did I explain enough in the conclusion?" I asked Mom. "Is Dad going to make it in time?"

"He'll be there. Your presentation is great, Danny. I'm so proud of all your hard work. You know, even if you don't win first place, it's okay. The speech won't be so bad now that you know about BRAVE."

"Yeah, I guess so. But I still want to win."

| Chapter 21 |

What To Do

The gymnasium was transformed into a humongous science room. Boy, was it crowded! There were rows and rows of tables with projects displayed by grade. Most teachers made the science contest mandatory, so that meant everyone had to participate, whether they wanted to or not. Not only were all the students there, but also their families, and many judges. Chaos filled the room as everyone hurried to put the final touches on their projects.

All we had to do was set up our bridge by the board with all our pictures and attach the typed report. I had spent extra time on that report, and it was absolutely perfect. I browsed around a little. The other projects didn't seem to have as much information and detail work as ours. *There's no way we can lose!* I thought.

Jack came in with our suspension bridge model. The next few seconds seemed to happen in slow motion.

Jack leaned to the side to let Mark go by with his water cycle replica. Then Sam came by a little too fast with his race car experiment and bumped into Mark. Raising his arms up to avoid Sam, Mark hit Jack on the head with his water cycle. Jack tried to step to the side and tripped on his own shoelace. He fell down hard, and our bridge broke into pieces all over the gymnasium floor!

There was a sudden hush in the crowd around us. Then several kids and some parents came over to help pick up the pieces. I stood there, frozen, wanting to cry. We couldn't replace that bridge! It took us most of the week to build it. Mark's and Sam's projects were both still in one piece, though.

I was worried about what to do now. I wandered around the gymnasium like a zombie, thinking that it was all for nothing, all that hard work. I stopped when I reached Jack's grandpa, resting on a folding chair. Sitting down beside him, I put my head in my hands.

He put his hand on my shoulder and said, "You know you've done well, Danny. So get out there now and be brave!"

Realizing there was nothing else I could do, I got up and walked over to Jack. I knew he felt bad because I wanted to win so much.

"Um, Jack." I said, "how about next time you make sure your *shoes* are ready before you leave the house. You know, be ready and victory's easy? I think that applies to tying your shoes too." He looked up at me and started to grin.

Then we both laughed.

Mark appeared to be truly sorry for the accident and said he would tell the judges that our bridge looked great. I think he was impressed by our work and was kind of rooting for us. I'm not so sure about Sam, but at least he did say he was sorry.

We spent the rest of the time setting up our display. We were ready with everything, even though we didn't have the bridge. Most of the judging was based on your observation, experiment, and conclusion. Having a model to present wasn't required, but we did the extra work because we wanted to win. Hopefully, we showed enough through our pictures and report. All we had to do now was wait for the judging.

Chapter 22

And The Winner Is...

The time finally arrived. Jack, Gramps, Mom, and I stood together to hear the judges' decision. They announced that for the first time in the school's history, they had a tie. "The first place winners are Mark and Maya's Water Cycle Project, and Danny and Jack's Bridge Design. We will have an identical trophy made for the co-winning team."

When I turned around, there was my brother Nick with Dad.

"Hey, nice going," Nick said, slapping me on the back.

Wow, I couldn't believe Nick said something nice to me!

I introduced Dad to Gramps and Jack. This was the best day of my life! When we won, Gramps gave the biggest smile I'd ever seen. It was like *he* had won the contest. Jack was so happy, too, not just because of winning, but to see his grandpa excited about something again.

Even though I was excited about winning, I realized that I didn't care about the speech anymore. Jack and Gramps had been right. I decided that nothing was as bad as it seemed when I remembered to be brave.

| Epilogue |

Boy, I sure learned a lot from the science project that year. Not just about bridges, but about trying new things and stuff. Eventually I did have to give a speech in the spring. I made sure I was prepared by rehearsing it about a million times. Walking up there was a little scary, but once I got started, it was a lot easier than I thought it would be.

Some things are still pretty hard for me, like when I took that claymation camp over the summer and I didn't know a single person in the class. It was worth it, though. We got to make our own stop-motion animated claymation videos. All the work was done by the kids—making the clay models, planning, videotaping, and the final editing. They ended up showing our work on community television. I'm glad now that I got all the information and decided to give it a chance.

When we had outdoor camp, it was hard because we had to stay overnight for four nights. We each got our own piece of land called a study plot where we learned about plants, soil, and water. There were hiking trails and some neat waterfalls. But the most fun was having campfires at night with skits and stories. It's good that I didn't try to get out of it, because it was a lot of fun.

I'm even on a lacrosse team now. At first I wasn't sure about it, but I found out it was a lot like soccer and hockey mixed into one sport. I'm a midfielder and I'm getting good at fast breaks and strategy. It's been great because I made a lot of good friends on the team.

I don't know if I'd have done any of these things before I got to know Jack and his grandpa. BRAVE really does apply to everything in life. All you have to do is be ready ahead of time. Now, whenever I have to tackle something hard, I always remember to be brave.

Be Ready And Victory's Easy

| Note to Parents |

Our "hero" in the story, Danny, suffers from symptoms of social anxiety. Social anxiety involves an unreasonable fear of social situations. The person is afraid that he or she will act in a way that will call attention to him or herself, which could ultimately be humiliating or embarrassing.

Children with this problem are usually content to stick with what is known because it is safe. They are less interested in exploring new things. Rather than become excited by new things, they are much more likely to be scared. They may be shy around strangers and may not speak much to people outside the family. Ordering food in a restaurant, going to birthday parties, talking to adults, starting a conversation, reading aloud in front of the class, and asking a teacher for help are just some of the many ways social anxiety might impact a child's life.

When you see your child become anxious, refuse to participate, or miss out on fun activities, it can be heart-breaking. Also, it can be frustrating when you have to reassure your child and try to help them cope, over and over again. You may not know what to do or where to turn for help.

This book was written to help parents and children learn more about what it is like for someone to be anxious much of the time. For some children, it can be beneficial to read about someone going through similar experiences or feeling similar feelings. Hopefully, your child will benefit from the story of *BRAVE*, about a boy's struggle and ultimate triumph over conflict in his life due to social anxiety.

— Jenne R. Henderson, Ph.D.

| Recommended Books |

Freeing Your Child From Anxiety: Powerful, Practical Solutions to Overcome Your Child's Fears, Worries, and Phobias, Tamar E. Chansky, Broadway, 2004.

The Anxiety Cure for Kids: A Guide For Parents, Elizabeth Dupont Spencer, Robert L. Dupont and Caroline M. Dupont, Wiley, 2003.

Worried No More—Second Edition: Help and Hope for Anxious Children, Aureen Wagner, Lighthouse Press, Inc., 2nd edition 2005.

The Shyness and Social Anxiety Workbook, Martin M. Antony and Richard P. Swinson, New Harbinger Publications, 2008.

Who Moved My Cheese for Kids, Spencer Johnson and Steve Pileggi, Penguin Young Readers Group, 2003.

Raising Your Spirited Child: A Guide for Parents Whose Child is More Intense, Sensitive, Perceptive, Persistent, Energetic, Mary Sheedy Kurcinka, HarperCollins Publishers, 2006.

Helping Your Anxious Child: A Step-by-Step Guide for Parents, Ronald M. Rapee, Susan Spence, Vanessa Cobham, and Ann Wignall, New Harbinger Publications; 1st edition, 2000.

| Acknowledgements |

We would like to thank Mrs. Angelique Harold and her 2006–2007 5th grade class at Scholls Heights Elementary for their initial enthusiasm for our story. Margaret McCloskey, M.D. for her comments and encouragement. Nancy Osa for her help with editing. We would also like to thank our families for their support.